THE SECRET EXPLORERS
AND THE ICE AGE ADVENTURE

CONTENTS

Chapter One
A CAMPING TRIP

Tamiko straightened the last tent peg and dusted off her hands. She admired the tent that she and her mom had just put up.

"There we go," she said with a smile.

Tamiko's mom set down some firewood. "So do you like the pattern?" she asked.

Tamiko stroked one of the dinosaurs printed on the tent flap: a velociraptor. "It's perfect!" she said with a grin. She was so glad she'd asked her mom to buy it.

Tamiko had always loved dinosaurs and prehistoric creatures. That was one of the reasons she and her mom were on vacation in the Japanese countryside, up in the hills near where they lived. Tamiko couldn't wait to explore the nearby cliffs, where she might find fossils or bones from animals that had lived millions of years ago.

"Do you want to light the campfire?" her mom asked. Tamiko stared at the box of matches that her mom was holding out to her. "With those?" she said.

"Unless you want to do it the old-fashioned way and rub two sticks together!" said her mom.

Tamiko took the box. "People in ancient times used stones to light fires, too," she said. "They struck two flints together to make a spark."

"Matches are easier," said her mom. "But you need to be careful. Remember, it's safer if you strike the match away from you."

Tamiko tried to strike a match down the rough side of the box, angling it away from her just the way her mom had said. She snapped the first one. The second one leaped to life but quickly sputtered out. The third one didn't strike at all.

"Maybe the matches got wet," said her mom, frowning. "Let's try again later. Now, who wants an untoasted marshmallow?"

"Me!" shouted Tamiko.

As her mom ducked through the dinosaur tent flap, Tamiko noticed a light out of the corner of her eye.

A glowing compass was shining on the face of a nearby rock. North, south, east, and west gleamed and flickered. The compass matched the badge that Tamiko was wearing. The sign of the Secret Explorers! There must be a mission!

The Secret Explorers were kids from all over the world with different special areas of expertise. Tamiko was their dinosaur and prehistory expert. She jumped to her feet and hurried over. Immediately, a shining door appeared on the rock.

With a buzz of excitement, Tamiko stepped through the door, into the dazzling light. Wind rushed through her hair. When the light faded, Tamiko found herself in the familiar surroundings of the Exploration Station. It was just as she remembered—the bank of computers set into the wall, the comfy sofas, the map of the world in the center of the floor, and the great domed ceiling showing all the stars of the Milky Way. Glass cases ranged around the room, displaying objects the Secret Explorers had collected on their missions, including feathers, seeds, meteorites, and fossils.

"Tamiko, here!" she called, and skipped over to the sofas to wait for the others.

Glowing doors appeared all around the room as the rest of the Secret Explorers arrived.

"Gustavo, here!" called a boy with dark curly hair, sauntering into the room with a grin. Gustavo was from Brazil, and was the history explorer.

"Connor, here!" A boy came in, pushing his wet hair out of his eyes. Connor was the marine explorer, he and came from the United States.

"Kiki, here!" Kiki had a smear of engine oil on her face, which made Tamiko smile. Kiki was the technology explorer, and she was from Ghana.

"Ollie, here!" called a blond boy with an Australian accent. His area of expertise was

the rainforests.

"Roshni, here!" announced a girl with a long shiny black braid, jogging into the Exploration Station and gazing at the stars on the domed ceilings. Roshni was from India, and she was the team's space explorer.

"Cheng, here!" Cheng had two rocks in his hands and a smile as wide as the Grand Canyon. He was the geology explorer from China.

The last to arrive was a tall girl wearing a hairband decorated with felt leaves. "Leah, here!" she called. Leah was British, and her specialty was biology.

"Good to see you, guys!" said Ollie. "What do you think our mission is?"

A light started glowing on the map of the world on the floor.

"Where's that?" said Gustavo as the Secret Explorers gathered around.

"Those are the Ural Mountains in Russia," said Tamiko.

A screen appeared, showing a boy dressed in a furry outfit. Their mission must be to help him somehow! Tamiko crossed her fingers. *I hope the Exploration Station chooses me!* she thought.

"Yes!" she cheered as her compass badge lit up.

"Oh wow, me too?" said Ollie in surprise as his own badge lit up as well. "Do they have rainforests in Russia?"

Ollie was a surprising choice. But the Exploration Station was never wrong.

Tamiko and Ollie grinned and high-fived each other.

"Ready when you are," said Leah, settling down at one of the Exploration Station computers. "Let's get this show on the road!"

"Remember, we're here if you need any help," added Roshni.

Kiki pressed a button beside the computers. The floor began to open. An ancient-looking go-kart rose from beneath the ground, its chipped red paint looking extra ratty in the overhead lights.

"Hey, Beagle," said Ollie cheerfully, patting the rusty old steering wheel. "Looking as good as ever!"

Tamiko laughed as she climbed into the old machine beside Ollie. The Beagle was the Secret Explorer's special mission vehicle. It wouldn't look like a creaky old go-kart for long. She wondered what sort of vehicle she and Ollie would have for their mission!

"Let's GO!" cried Ollie.

The Exploration Station vanished in a burst of bright light as the Beagle started to accelerate. The steering wheel juddered beneath Tamiko's hands as the Beagle transformed. A comfy seat appeared underneath her. The dented metal steering wheel began to lengthen into handlebars. Tamiko realized that Ollie was no longer sitting beside her, but behind.

With a sudden whoosh and a judder,

the light and the wind stopped. Tamiko blinked. It was very cold, and extremely dark.

Where were they?

Chapter Two
A MYSTERIOUS BOY

Tamiko blinked, adjusting to the dark. She felt something soft brush her chin. Looking down, she saw she was wearing a jacket and pants made of fake fur, and her hands were cozy inside furry gloves. She was glad for the warmth. This place was cold.

Ollie was wearing fur, too. He looked a

little like a bear, Tamiko thought with a giggle as she looked over her shoulder at her passenger.

"Great look, Beagle!" Ollie said. It had transformed into a sandy-colored ATV, with big wheels, a touchscreen dashboard, and a padded seat.

Tamiko switched on the Beagle's headlights. Now she could see a wide-open landscape in front of them, dotted with scrubby undergrowth. Far in the distance was a range of cliffs.

Ollie hopped off the Beagle and crouched down in the beam of the headlights. "Sedge and grass," he confirmed, running his hand over the small green plants on the ground. "So where's this person we're meant to be helping?"

There was no sign of the boy the Exploration Station had shown them. "We'd better look for him," said Tamiko.

Ollie climbed back onto the Beagle and Tamiko revved the engine. The Beagle gave a throaty roar as they moved away, heading toward the cliffs.

The landscape was vast, silent, and empty. Tamiko had never experienced anywhere like it. Back home, there were people everywhere. In this place, Tamiko felt as if she and Ollie were the only living creatures for hundreds of miles.

Well, maybe not the only living creatures. Eyes glinted eerily in the headlights as the Beagle purred along. It was too dark to tell what kind of animals they belonged to, but they seemed small to Tamiko. Rodents, maybe.

They were approaching the dark cliffs now. A distant sound traveled through the silent night air toward them.

"What's that?" Ollie said.

Tamiko turned off the Beagle's engine. There it was again—a howl, echoing across the empty landscape.

"A dog, maybe?" she suggested.

"Let's check it out," said Ollie.

He hopped off the Beagle and dug through the storage boxes attached to the back. The Exploration Station always made sure the Secret Explorers had everything they needed for their missions. Sure enough, Ollie found two flashlights. He handed one to Tamiko.

The howling sounded louder than ever. Tamiko felt the hairs rise on the back of her neck.

"It's coming from over there," she said, pointing her flashlight beam at the cliffs. "Come on."

Tamiko and Ollie walked toward the sound. Soon, Tamiko could see the shape of an animal with its head raised to the sky.

"Tamiko, that's not a dog," Ollie said quietly. "It's a wolf!"

The wolf turned its large gray head. It stared at Ollie and Tamiko with wide yellow eyes. Then it started trotting away.

Tamiko relaxed. "I think it's tame," she said.

The wolf stopped and looked back over its shoulder at Tamiko and Ollie.

"It wants us to follow it," Ollie said.

They picked their way through rocks and scrub toward a tumbled heap of rocks at the base of a cliff. The wolf trotted on, looking back every now and then to make sure Ollie and Tamiko were still there.

The ground rose a little. Tamiko spotted a figure lying motionless on the ground below the tumbled rocks. A boy in furs...

"Ollie!" she gasped. "Quickly!"

The wolf sat down as Tamiko and Ollie carefully turned the boy over. It was definitely the boy from the video. He was dressed in thick, ragged furs.

"He's unconscious," said Ollie, checking the boy's pulse.

There was a nasty graze and a purple bump on the boy's forehead. It looked like he'd slipped on the rocks and knocked himself out.

"That looks bad," Tamiko said, feeling worried. "We should call the others."

They ran back to the Beagle. Tamiko turned on the ignition and the engine jumped to life. She tapped the digital screen set into the handlebars. A picture appeared, showing the others gathered around one of the Exploration Station computers.

"We need medical advice." said Tamiko, and explained the situation.

Leah quickly tapped something into her keyboard. "Clean up the graze and keep him warm," she said, checking her screen.

"And when he comes around, ask him some questions," Roshni put in. "To check whether he's confused. Like, ask him his name, and how many fingers you're holding up. That kind of thing."

"Thanks guys," said Tamiko. "Over and out."

"Good luck!" called the other Explorers, just as the dashboard screen winked out.

When they got back, the boy was still sprawled at the foot of the rocks. The night air was cold, and frost sparkled on the ground.

"Leah said we have to keep him warm,"

said Ollie, shivering.

"We should find shelter," said Tamiko. Pointing her flashlight at the cliff face behind the fallen rocks, she spotted a dark crack. "Over there, Ollie. Do you see it?" she said.

"A cave!" Ollie exclaimed.

Tamiko took the boy's shoulders and

Ollie took his feet. He was heavy, and as they carried him into the cave and set him down carefully. The wolf padded anxiously after them, and lay down with its big head on its paws in the cave mouth. It whined softly. It was clear that the wolf was worried about the boy.

"We'll do our best for your friend—OK, buddy?" Tamiko told the wolf.

While Ollie ran back to the Beagle to fetch a flask of water to wash the boy's wound, Tamiko gathered some wood to build a fire. There were plenty of small sticks and larger twigs lying on the ground among the shrubs. Tamiko stacked them carefully outside the cave mouth, leaving enough space for the air to move through the twigs, just as her mom had shown her with their campfire.

"Did you happen to see any matches in the Beagle?" Tamiko asked Ollie, when he came running back.

Ollie shook his head. "No, sorry."

"I guess it's time to put some prehistoric knowledge to the test," she said. She started picking up stones.

"What are you doing?" asked Ollie, who had started washing the boy's wound.

Tamiko pushed her dark hair out of her eyes. "Looking for flints," she explained. "We can light the fire with them. Aha, got one! And another!"

Finding the flints was easy. But no

matter how hard Tamiko tried to strike them together, she couldn't make a spark. She dropped them in frustration.

"So much for keeping him warm," she said gloomily.

"Don't worry," said Ollie. "We've got our patient into shelter and his outfit is pretty cozy. Now we just have to wait for him to wake up."

Tamiko settled down with her back against the cave wall. The wolf sat up, its eyes glinting in the moonlight.

"Who is this boy, do you think?" Ollie asked into the silence.

"I don't know," Tamiko admitted. "But if it's our mission to take care of him, then we will."

She gazed at the moonlit landscape outside the cave. Something about the stillness and emptiness of this place seemed odd. It felt almost as if they were on another planet.

Tamiko must have nodded off, because the next thing she knew, bright sunbeams were flooding into the cave. She squinted into the orange light. Ollie was asleep, lying curled up beside the boy in furs. The wolf was nowhere to be seen. *I guess you're out hunting.*

Turning her head, she caught sight of something painted on the wall of the cave, picked out in the bright morning sunlight.

The painting showed a herd of large, shaggy, orange animals with curved tusks. Mammoths!

Tamiko knew the giant elephants had been extinct for at least ten thousand years.

But the colors in the cave painting were as bright and fresh as if they had been painted yesterday.

She shook Ollie awake.

"I know where we are!" she said with excitement as Ollie rubbed the sleep from his eyes. "Ollie, we've gone back in time—to the Ice Age!"

Chapter Three
THE ICE AGE

"Wow," Ollie breathed as he and Tamiko stared at the cave painting.

The painting showed a herd of mammoths standing by a frozen river. Their tusks were huge and sharp, and their trunks curved down and then up again. Tamiko could almost hear the creak of ice pushing against the painted riverbanks.

"So when was the Ice Age?" asked Ollie. "Are we talking dinosaur times?"

Tamiko shook her head. "After the dinosaurs. But it's still a really long time in the past. We could be anywhere between eleven thousand years ago, or a lot longer."

"Cool!" Ollie exclaimed.

"That's why it's so cold," said Tamiko. "During the Ice Age, a huge sheet of ice was spreading across the world."

Ollie gazed out of the cave. "There's not much ice or snow out there," he said, pointing to the wide open landscape with its waving green grasses and rocks.

"We must be in the area called the 'mammoth steppe'," Tamiko guessed. "It covered much of Russia, Asia, parts of Europe, and North America. It was cold, but it wasn't covered in ice and snow like other places were."

"That explains the mammoths!" Ollie exclaimed. "A place like this is full of grass and food for them to eat. Unlike the icy places."

"Exactly," Tamiko agreed.

A groan from the boy made them both turn around. He was beginning to stir.

"We should hide the Beagle," said Ollie suddenly. "We don't want to freak this guy out. He's never seen anything like it."

They quickly ran out of the cave and down through the rocks and scrub to where they'd left the Beagle the night before. Gathering armfuls of foliage, they covered the Beagle so that it

blended in with its surroundings. The ATV
BEEPED sadly.

"It's not for long, Beagle," Tamiko
promised, patting the vehicle's
sleek handlebars.

When they returned to the cave, the
boy was trying to sit up.

"Hey, take it easy," Ollie said, kneeling

down and supporting his back. "You had a
nasty fall last night."

"How are you feeling?" Tamiko asked.
"Do you feel sick? Dizzy?"

"How many fingers am I holding up?"
asked Ollie, extending four fingers.

The boy rubbed his forehead. "My head

hurts a bit, but I'm fine. And that's four fingers. Who are you?"

There was a sudden skittering of paws. The wolf bounded into the cave with its long pink tongue hanging out of its mouth. It covered the boy in warm, wet licks.

'Hey, don't worry!" said the boy, laughing and hugging the wolf. "I'm fine! Where did you find these two?"

The wolf gave a joyful bark and ran around the cave, tail wagging.

"She's named Fang, by the way," said the boy. "And I'm Leaf."

Tamiko introduced herself and Ollie. "We were just, er, passing by when Fang found us and led us to you," she explained.

"Thank you," said the boy. He frowned. "I've never seen you before. Where did you come from?"

Ollie and Tamiko shared a glance. How do you tell someone that you are from thousands of years into the future?

"A place very, umm, far from here," Ollie improvised.

"I love your wolf," Tamiko added.

"I found Fang when she was a cub," Leaf said, rubbing his wolf's ears. "She's been with me her whole life." He suddenly looked alarmed. "Did you see anyone else when you were traveling? Fang and I were hunting and we got separated from the rest of my people. And then I guess I fell, and..."

His eyes widened. "They'll be so far away by now, following the mammoths! How will Fang and I find them by ourselves?"

Tamiko and Ollie shared a look. Tamiko knew Ollie was thinking the same thing as her. Their mission was clear. They had to help Leaf find his people!

"We'll come with you," Ollie offered.

Leaf was delighted. "You will? Thank you!" He stood up, wincing a little from the bump on his forehead. Fang skipped around his legs. "We should go, before they get too far ahead of us."

"So which way do you think they went?" Tamiko asked.

Leaf pointed at the cave painting. "The mammoths always cross the river at this bend, a little distance from here. If we find the mammoths, then we'll find my people."

"That's a really beautiful painting," said Tamiko.

"I painted it," said Leaf with pride.

Tamiko and Ollie stared at the boy in amazement.

Leaf nodded. "I've painted others, in all the places where we hunt," he explained. "It's a way of remembering."

"Like writing in a diary," said Ollie.

Leaf looked puzzled. "What is writing?"

"Never mind," said Tamiko, laughing. "Come on. We have some mammoths to find!"

Chapter Four
ACROSS THE STEPPE

Leaf, Fang, Tamiko, and Ollie trekked together across the wide steppe, leaving the cave behind. Tamiko could tell Leaf and Fang were familiar with the landscape and the route. They were fast, too. She and Ollie followed more slowly, picking their way through the sedge and the grasses.

Ollie had a spring in his step as he walked beside Tamiko, pointing out all the plants. His botanical expertise meant he knew exactly what they were looking at.

"That's a conifer over there," he explained, pointing at a row of spiky-looking trees. He bent down and stroked a patch of soft emerald-green growth clinging to the rocks. "And this is moss. Feel it! It's like a rabbit's fur."

Tamiko stroked the moss. She could see what Ollie meant.

Leaf and Fang were almost specks in the distance now. Tamiko and Ollie picked up their pace, not wanting to get lost. The air was pure and clean, and Tamiko took deep lungfuls.

Dotted around the landscape, she saw animals grazing on the plain.

"That looks like a rhino!" said Ollie, pointing at a large, hairy creature with two horns on the front of its broad head. "Only with fur."

"It's a woolly rhinoceros," said Tamiko, grinning.

She couldn't believe she was seeing the ancient animal for herself, with its tufty brown feet and huge, shaggy flanks. Like mammoths, she only knew woolly rhinos from books. There were other animals too, grazing peacefully under the wide skies of the steppe: sturdy-looking horses with bristling manes, and great bison with high humps on their shoulders and wicked-looking horns on the sides of their heads.

"So why are Leaf's people following the mammoths?" Ollie asked.

"Humans at this time were hunter-gatherers," Tamiko explained. "Farming hadn't been developed yet, so humans had to hunt or find everything that they ate. This meant they were always on the move. They hunted mammoths for food, and to use their fur and bones to make what they needed. So if the mammoths moved, the people did too."

"That's why Leaf didn't ask any more questions about where we were from," Ollie guessed. "Because no one's really from anywhere."

Tamiko laughed. "I guess that's true."

Ollie rested his hands on his hips. 'That's why he's so much fitter and faster than we are, too," he said. "He's used to always being on the move."

Leaf and Fang bounded into view. Leaf was carrying an armful of greenery.

"Food," he explained, placing his finds on a rock. "We need to eat to keep up our strength. Help yourselves."

Tamiko and Ollie stared at the vegetables and fruit. Tamiko recognized tiny tomatoes and spiky cucumbers. There were also stubby carrots— about as long as Tamiko's pinkie.

Tamiko took a tiny purple carrot and bit into it. It wasn't as sweet as the carrots she was used to. She glanced at Ollie, who was chewing his way through a little cucumber with a look of concentration on his face. It looked as if the cucumbers didn't taste like the modern version either. It would be a few more thousand years before humans perfected the tastiest fruit and vegetables by farming them and selecting the seeds to improve their crops.

Fang waited patiently for them to finish their meal.

Leaf wiped his mouth with the back of his hand. "Not much farther to the river bend now," he said. "We might see the mammoths and my people there."

They trekked on. The air grew colder, sweeping around them in icy gusts. Tamiko shivered in her furs. Even though there was no snow here, the tips of the grasses and shrubs were white and frosty.

"Just over this rise and we should see the river," Leaf said, picking up his pace eagerly. "The mammoths always... oh!"

Tamiko and Ollie stopped beside Leaf at the top of the rise.

"I can't see any mammoths," said Ollie, shading his eyes.

Tamiko stared at the river bend.

She recognized it from Leaf's cave painting, the way it cut through the landscape in a curving loop. But today it looked different. Instead of being covered in ice, as Leaf had expected, most of the water was fast and flowing.

"It's much wider than I remember," said Leaf, looking dismayed. "And a lot of the ice has already melted. The mammoths usually cross on the ice. So do we. But there's no way any of us could cross now."

Tamiko looked up and down the riverbanks. There was no sign of the huge animals—no footprints, no trampled

grasses. Nothing. Just the water, sweeping past.

"So how did they cross?" she said.

Leaf lifted his hands in the air. "I don't know," he said anxiously. "And if I can't find the crossing place, I can't find the mammoths . . ." Ollie finished the sentence for him. ". . . and you can't find your people!"

Chapter Five
OLLIE THE TRACKER

Leaf stared out at the river. He looked so worried. Beside him, Fang whined softly and licked his hand.

There were a few patches of solid ice by the riverbanks, but Tamiko could see where the ice was thin, showing the water running fast beneath it. It would be dangerous to cross. She made some quick calculations. If the snow was melting, then they were somewhere toward the end of the Ice Age, when the great ice sheets that covered most of Europe were melting and receding. It reminded her uncomfortably of the way the climate was changing in the present day.

Leaf sat down on a nearby rock with his head bowed.

"Cheer up," said Ollie, laying a hand on Leaf's shoulder. "We can still do this – together. The mammoths must have taken a different route, that's all. If we can track them, then we'll find your people. I'm a pretty good tracker," he added.

Tamiko knew that Ollie tracked animals in the Australian outback all the time. She hoped he could do the same here, on the Ice Age steppe.

Leaf sighed. "I guess we can give it a try," he said.

Ollie hunkered down and studied the ground around their feet. After a moment, he got up again, and started heading slowly along the riverbank.

Tamiko and Leaf followed, with Fang trotting at Leaf's heels.

Ollie kept stopping and studying the ground. Tamiko guessed he was looking for footprints. She wondered how big a mammoth footprint would be...

"I've got something!" Ollie suddenly called.

Leaf ran over to the patch of wet ground where Ollie was kneeling. "Yes!" he exclaimed. "The mammoths have definitely passed through here. And recently, too!"

Tamiko ran over also. Ollie had found a footprint, clearly marked in the mud by their feet—as round and large as a plate.

"And look at this tree!" said Ollie, pointing

a little farther along. "Lots of leaves have been picked off. Looks like a mammoth stopped for a snack!"

Tamiko could imagine a long trunk reaching up and stripping leaves from the branches.

Leaf clapped his hands in delight. "I'm so

glad you're with me! We're going the right way for sure."

Ollie looked around at the empty steppe. "But I don't know where they went next," he confessed. "I can't see any more clues."

They could still hear the river, but otherwise there was silence all around them.

No grazing woolly rhinoceros, very little vegetation, and definitely no mammoths. The hills rolled away in the distance, clear and dusted with snow. Tamiko felt a little shiver. It was easy to feel very alone in this environment.

"Now that we know for sure the mammoths came this way, I'm sure I can find them," Leaf said. He looked a lot more hopeful than he had before.

He began moving with his eyes sweeping from left to right. Tamiko and Ollie followed doubtfully. The ground was rocky and hard, and it would be almost impossible to spot tracks.

After a few minutes Leaf gave a yell. "Broken grass!" he cried. "Flattened by mammoths. See?"

The little patch of scrubby grass was bent

and crushed, but it was so small that Tamiko and Ollie would have missed it by themselves. Leaf ran on, calling out other clues as they went—stones that had skittered away under tramping mammoth feet, a tiny twig that lay snapped in half. Fang trotted loyally by his side, sniffing the ground and listening with one ear cocked to the wind.

"This is amazing," Ollie whispered to Tamiko as they followed Leaf. "I could never track like him."

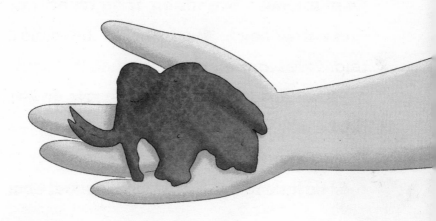

"Ice Age people relied on tracking," Tamiko murmured back. "If they lost the mammoths, they lost their food. I think Leaf learned how to track from his parents."

"Hey," said Leaf suddenly. He stopped and picked something out of a little shrub. "Look at this!"

He held out something pale and small, carved out of bone. There were four legs, and a tiny sweeping trunk. It looked like . . .

"Is that a mammoth?" Tamiko gasped. She knew that Ice Age people had made a lot of art, but it was still amazing to see.

Leaf grinned. "Birch makes these," he said. "He's my mother's brother. He must have dropped it. We are definitely on the right track!"

Even Tamiko could now see the lines in the dust and grass which marked the

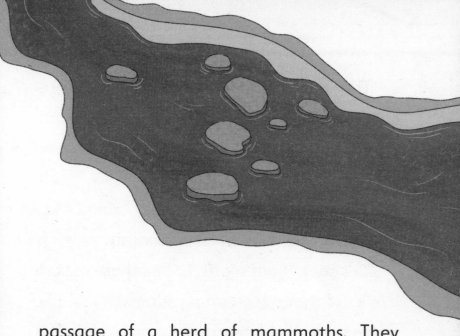

passage of a herd of mammoths. They moved onward as the ground rose away from the river and then dipped back down again, through a steep gully and down to the edge of the water once more.

Tamiko saw at once that the river was narrower here, and easier to cross. The water ran fast, squeezing through the rocky banks with a roar and a hiss.

"Over there!" cried Leaf, pointing to the far side. "That tree. It has a broken branch."

The new wood of the splintered tree gleamed bright and pale in the daylight.

"The mammoths broke that when they crossed," said Leaf.

"So we have to cross this too?" said Ollie, looking at the river a little anxiously.

"It's easy," Leaf scoffed. "See those rocks? We'll use them as stepping stones."

Tamiko could see that a row of jagged

rocks zigzagged neatly across the river, each stone barely a jump away from its neighbor.

"You go first, Tamiko!" Leaf suggested. "We'll follow you."

The stones looked easy enough to cross from the shore. But Tamiko soon found that they were wet and slippery with river spray. She wobbled on the first stone, and almost

missed the second all together. But slowly, with Ollie following behind, she jumped from rock to rock, and tried not to look at the cold water rushing below her feet. Behind them both, the Ice Age boy made it look easy, hopping from one stone to the next.

Fang was the last to cross. She hesitated halfway. It was clear that she didn't like the rushing river.

"You can do it, Fang!" called Leaf, looking back over his shoulder and holding out his hands in encouragement.

Tamiko and Ollie joined in. "Come on, girl! Not much farther!" they called.

Fang jumped to the next rock. But she had misjudged the distance. With a yelp and a frantic scrabble of paws, she slipped and fell into the raging water!

Chapter Six
A RESCUE

"FANG!" cried Leaf.

The wolf was floundering in the water, paddling hard, but the current was strong. Tamiko could see that she was struggling.

"I'm coming, Fang!" shouted Leaf.

Fang whimpered, getting disoriented as the water whirled her around. Leaf scrambled back over the rocks, stretching down, trying to reach her and grab her fur. But he couldn't reach far enough.

"We have to rescue her!" shouted Leaf. "Please help me! I can't lose Fang!"

Ollie turned back, scrambling over to where Leaf was leaning down over the whirling water.

Tamiko was just a few jumps away from dry land now. Should she go back? But then she had an idea. She jumped as fast as she could to the shore, and grabbed one of the branches that had been snapped off by the passing mammoths.

Hoisting it over her shoulder, she ran back to the stepping stones, hopping carefully from rock to rock.

"Good thinking, Tamiko!" Ollie exclaimed when she reached them.

Tamiko knelt down on the rock and reached out as far as she could with the branch. "Come on, Fang!" she shouted. "Come on, girl! Grab the branch!"

Fang was getting tired. She tried to scrabble toward the branch as it dangled on

the water, but she couldn't reach it.

"It's no good; it's not long enough," Leaf said helplessly.

"Hold hands," said Ollie suddenly. "That way we can reach a bit farther!"

He grabbed Tamiko's hand, then held out his other hand to Leaf. Leaf took it, and wrapped his free arm around the rock to anchor them. Tamiko grasped Ollie's hand tightly, and stretched out a bit farther with the branch. Farther... just a little farther... if

she let go of Ollie, she would fall in...

Fang reared out of the water one final time, splashing with her paws. Tamiko felt a sudden tug as the wolf fastened her mouth around the branch.

"Yes!" she shouted in triumph. "Come on, Fang! Paddle!"

She heaved back, finding her own balance again. Ollie grabbed the branch now. So did Leaf.

Together they heaved and pulled the wolf toward them. Finally, with one last splash, Fang pulled herself free of the swirling water and scrambled on to the rock.

"We did it!" Ollie cheered.

Leaf threw his arms around the sopping wet wolf, who promptly shook herself from nose to tail and drenched them all, her tail wagging hard.

"Oh Fang!" cried Leaf, laughing and burying his face in the wolf's wet neck. "You're safe! We've got you! Don't ever scare me like that again!"

They all sat on the riverbank for a few minutes after Fang's rescue to catch their breath. Leaf thanked Tamiko and Ollie over and over again. Fang thanked them, too, in her own way, by licking their faces with her long tongue.

Eventually, they all stood up to continue on the trail of the mammoths. The trail was very distinct now. Tamiko even spotted piles of fresh mammoth dung. Her heart leaped to think that she might see a real-life mammoth soon.

"There they are!" said Leaf suddenly.

Tamiko squinted eagerly into the bright winter light, shading her eyes to get a better view. "I can see them!" she exclaimed.

Even at this distance, the mammoth herd looked enormous. There must have been thirty animals or more, all moving slowly together, their trunks swaying. Their orange fur was long and shaggy, and blew around in the wind. The adults' huge tusks glinted in the sun. There were even several youngsters, clustering around the adults.

The sound of trumpeting floated toward them. The mammoths were acting strangely, swinging their trunks high and clustering close together.

"Something is scaring them," Tamiko guessed. She felt a little prickle of fear as she glanced around. There were some scary predators during the Ice Age—cave lions and bears.

"Maybe they can smell us," suggested Ollie.

"We're too far away," said Leaf. "Maybe they're smelling my people."

Of course, thought Tamiko. Humans are predators, too.

"Or something else," Leaf added. "A bear, maybe."

Ollie looked nervous. He clearly didn't want to meet any predator that scared something as big as a mammoth.

The herd moved around restlessly, trumpeting and making small, half-hearted charges at one another. Then, as if someone had given a signal, they began to move on. They moved fast for such big animals. It wasn't long before they were out of sight again, swaying over the horizon.

"We should rest and eat," suggested Leaf. "We won't lose them again. Can you build the fire? Fang and I will go hunting."

The boy and his wolf set off in search of food. Ollie and Tamiko gathered sticks, as Tamiko had done at the cave the previous night, and carefully stacked them in a pile. Tamiko found a couple of flints and tried to light the fire again, but she still couldn't do it. It was very frustrating.

Leaf reappeared, holding two long-legged hares. "Food!" he announced.

"We can't light the fire," Tamiko confessed.

Leaf grinned. "You don't have any moss," he said. "No moss, no fire!"

Tamiko wanted to kick herself. Of course—she needed something dry and small to start the flames!

Ollie quickly gathered up some dry moss and tucked it into the base of the piled wood. Then Leaf took two flints from the pouch on his belt, knelt down, and struck the stones together. On the third attempt, the spark leaped from the stones into the moss, where it started quietly smoldering. Cupping his hands around the tiny flame, Leaf blew gently until the flames

licked high enough
to reach the
small, dry twigs
at the base. In
no time at all,
the fire was red
and glowing.

"You did it!"
cheered Tamiko.

Leaf had a clay
pot tied around his
waist. He took it off and placed
it on the fire. Soon the air was filled
with the delicious sizzling smell of the
hares cooking.

Fang had laid down beside the fire
after hunting with Leaf, watching them
all with her bright eyes. Now, as they
finished their meal, she suddenly she sat up.

A soft growl came from her throat.

"What's the matter, Fang?" said Leaf, jumping up.

Fang stood up now, growling louder. Tamiko's stomach clenched.

Something was out there . . .

Chapter Seven
CAVE LION ALERT!

A frightened, high-pitched trumpeting wafted toward them.

"Is that a baby mammoth?" Tamiko asked.

Leaf nodded. "Sounds like it's in trouble. Let's see what's happening!"

They all hurried away from their

campsite toward the baby mammoth's cries. They ran fast, through the grassland and up and over a small ridge—and saw...

"Cave lions!" gasped Ollie.

A young mammoth was surrounded by a pack of hungry-looking cave lions. It was whirling around clumsily, lashing out with its little trunk. But each time it

turned its back on a cave lion, the frightening animal crept closer.

Tamiko couldn't bear to see the young animal in trouble. "We have to help!" she burst out.

Leaf looked surprised. "What for?"

"We can't just watch," said Tamiko. "It's so frightened!"

Leaf was still puzzled. "I've never heard of anyone helping a mammoth before," he said. Then he shrugged. "But you two helped me. So if this is important to you, I will help you. What do you want to do?"

The pack of cave lions was closing in on the frightened mammoth. There was no time to lose.

"Hey!" Tamiko shouted. She waved her arms. "Hey! Leave him alone!"

The snarling stopped. The cave lions turned their heads and stared at Tamiko with wild yellow eyes. The silence was terrifying.

"Now what?" said Ollie, a little shakily.

The biggest cave lion roared and showed its long yellow teeth. The muscles in its powerful back legs bunched up as it prepared to leap toward the them.

"Now we run," said Tamiko, sounding braver than she felt. "Back toward the campfire. Come on!"

She spun around and raced away, back down the ridge. Leaf ran too, swiftly and silently, with Fang bounding along beside him. Ollie pounded after them.

"This is crazy!" Ollie shouted. "Cave lions can run quicker than we can!"

"We don't have to run for long!" Tamiko shouted back. "I have a plan. Trust me!"

Behind them, the cave lions roared and gave chase. Back down the ridge... back through the grass...

Tamiko's legs felt weak. She stumbled and almost fell, but righted herself and kept going. There was a vicious roar just behind them...

And there it was. Their campfire, bright and fiery. Tamiko raced beyond the flames and finally stopped running. They were safe now.

"Animals hate fire," she panted at Ollie and Leaf. "Look."

Behind them, the cave lions yelped in terror at the sight and sound of the fire. Then, just as Tamiko had hoped, they whimpered, turned tail, and fled.

"I'm so glad your plan worked, Tamiko," Ollie said, laughing and gasping at the same time. "I really didn't want to be lion lunch!"

When they had caught their breath, they put out the fire. Leaf tied his cooking pot back to his belt. Then they set off, back toward the ridge, where they had last seen the baby mammoth. He was still there, trotting around and waving

his small trunk in the air.

Tamiko approached the baby animal very slowly. She didn't want to scare him. "Hey there," she said gently and held out her hand. "Are you OK, little guy?"

The baby made a squeaky little trumpeting sound, but it didn't run away. Tamiko came closer, speaking quietly. "Look at you, all alone," she said. "We need to find your mom, don't we?"

The little mammoth lowered his trunk and watched her curiously. Now Tamiko was close enough to reach out and touch the orange fur on its back. It felt smooth and oily. Tamiko knew that the oils in the mammoth's coat helped insulate it against the cold. She marveled at the feeling of the glossy fur under her fingers. She was actually touching an Ice Age mammal.

"Look," said Ollie. "The other mammoths are coming over to say hello!"

Tamiko turned to see the whole herd of mammoths heading toward them, bellowing and swinging their trunks. Their curved tusks were enormous.

Leaf's eyes widened. "Uh-oh," he said. "They're not coming to say hello. They think we're the ones who took the baby!"

The biggest mammoth of the herd flung up her trunk and roared in fury.

"Run!" yelled Leaf.

Her heart pounding, Tamiko raced after Ollie and Leaf.

When she glanced over her shoulder, she saw that the mammoths had broken into a furious, screaming charge.

It was a stampede!

Chapter Eight
STAMPEDE!

Tamiko, Ollie, and Leaf ran as fast as they could, away from the stampeding mammoths. Fang ran beside them, her ears pricked anxiously.

"Faster!" Leaf shouted over the furious trumpeting.

"I'm not used to running so much!"

Ollie complained, clutching his side.

Tamiko was breathing heavily, too. Here they were, running away from dangerous creatures for the second time! Ice Age people must have been really fit.

"We need to climb a tree," she gasped, running as hard as she could. "Over there!"

Some way in the distance was a clump of tall, spiky-looking conifers.

"Too far away," panted Ollie.

"We have no choice," said Leaf. "Come on!"

The mammoths were catching up. The ground shook with the thunderous sound of their huge feet and the air was full of their strong, earthy smell. Their small eyes glared and their ears flapped. Fang barked, encouraging the Explorers and Leaf as they ran. They were almost at the tree...

Tamiko flung herself at the lowest conifer branch and pulled herself up. Leaf swarmed up behind her, hauling Fang with him, as agile as a monkey.

"Come on, Ollie!" cried Tamiko, glancing over her shoulder.

The mammoths were almost on them. Ollie took a flying leap at a low-hanging branch and pulled himself off the ground.

"We need to get higher," Leaf urged, climbing up past Tamiko with Fang draped around his shoulders. "Mammoths can reach—"

"WHOA!" cried Tamiko as a mammoth swiped at a branch just below her. She scrambled farther up the tree, climbing hand over hand until she reached a safe spot more than halfway up the trunk.

They'd made it just in time. The mammoths stomped around below them, walloping the tree with their trunks and using their tusks as battering rams. It was both terrifying and amazing.

"Look at the size of those tusks!" Tamiko gasped, clinging on to her branch as the tree quivered. "They're too curved for stabbing, so they're using them to hit instead. Wow! And you can see the store of fat on their necks and shoulders, to keep them going if they can't find food!"

WHAM! WALLOP! The trunk creaked and groaned and shook.

"F-f-fascinating," stammered Ollie, clinging as tight as he could to his branch. "When will they go away?"

The herd paced around the bottom of the tree for a few more minutes, giving Tamiko an uninterrupted view of their furry orange backs and hard yellow tusks. The biggest mammoth gave a final snort of rage, tossed her head, and began to walk away. After a couple of moments the herd followed.

"The big mammoth must be the matriarch," Tamiko guessed. "The one who makes the decisions, like in a herd of elephants."

"Is it safe to climb down now?" Ollie said.

"All clear!" Leaf called, from somewhere near the top of the tree. "The mammoths have forgotten about us."

They climbed back down and set off cautiously, keeping a safe distance from the mammoths, who were once again walking together peacefully. Tamiko carefully avoided the piles of fresh dung on the ground as they followed the animals' swaying orange rumps.

Leaf suddenly gave a shout. "There! My people! We found them!"

In the distance, Tamiko saw a group of about twenty people gathered together, all wearing shaggy furs and skins.

A campfire sent up thin spirals of smoke into the sky.

Leaf broke into a run, waving and shouting at the group. Tamiko and Ollie followed.

"More running," Ollie sighed, but he was smiling. It was wonderful to know that they had found Leaf's people.

The smell of cooking meat wafted up Tamiko's nose as they got closer. She gazed in fascination at Leaf's people, all busy doing something: preparing skins, tending the fire, carving tools from bones. A group of men were making a tent from animal skins, stretching them tightly over frames lashed together with ropes made from grass fibers.

"Mama!" Leaf shouted, running faster. "Papa!"

Two people moved toward them, smiling widely.

Leaf's mom had the same smile as her son. "We thought we lost you!" she cried, holding out her arms.

Leaf tumbled into his mother's embrace. Leaf's dad grinned, tousled his son's hair, and rubbed Fang's ears as she frolicked around their legs.

"These are my friends," said Leaf, introducing Ollie and Tamiko. "I would never have found you if they hadn't helped me. And they saved Fang's life in the river!"

Leaf's father grasped Ollie's arm. "Thank you," he said sincerely. He did the same to Tamiko. "We were very worried. It's not safe out there alone."

Tamiko laughed. "So we discovered!"

"But you brought our son back to us," said Leaf's mother warmly. "How can we ever thank you?"

Leaf grinned. "Wait here," he told Tamiko and Ollie. "I want to give you something."

Tamiko and Ollie exchanged looks. What was Leaf planning?

It wasn't long before Leaf returned, with Fang beside him. He was holding a smooth, flat rock and what looked like a shell filled with . . .

"Paints!" Tamiko exclaimed.

"I made them," Leaf explained. "I ground

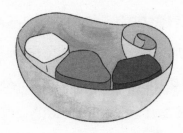

up different stones for the colors." He proudly showed Ollie and Tamiko three blocks of stone: charcoal for black, a yellowish rock, which Tamiko guessed was ocher, some reddish clay, and a chunk of white chalk. "Then I mixed them with plant sap and animal fat. That makes them stick. You can add water, too. It makes the paint last longer, but the colors aren't so strong."

He dipped his finger in the colors and

began to paint something on the smooth rock. He used black first, to make an outlined shape. Then it was yellow and red for the main colors. Finally Leaf added white. The white made the shapes almost pop out of the rock. It was a kind of magic.

"That's us!" Tamiko exclaimed. "Look, Ollie! You, me, Leaf... Fang, too!"

"And the baby mammoth!" Ollie said, laughing in amazement as he pointed at the distinctive shape of the little animal, with its small white tusks and long yellow-red fur.

"It's for you both," said Leaf, handing the rock to Tamiko. "To say thank you."

Tamiko sighed. Their mission was complete.

They said their goodbyes to Leaf and his family, and stroked Fang's ears one last time. Then, waving to the whole group, Tamiko and Ollie set off, back down the mammoth track.

"We've walked for ages since we left the Beagle," said Ollie a little anxiously as they crested the ridge where they had seen the baby mammoth and headed toward the rocky river pass. "It's going to take us ages to get back."

"Good news, Ollie," said Tamiko with a grin. "The Beagle's right here!"

A shiny, sandy-colored ATV came trundling toward them, **BEEPING** happily and flashing its lights.

"It must have tracked us," said Tamiko, laughing. "Good old Beagle!"

Ollie whooped and jumped on to the padded seat of the ATV. Tamiko took the front seat and twisted the throttle. With a roar, the Beagle zoomed into a beam of bright, pulsing light. Tamiko hung on tight.

With a final whoosh and a thud, they were back at the Exploration Station.

"You made it!" cheered Gustavo as everyone helped Ollie and Tamiko out of the Beagle.

"Mission accomplished," said Tamiko with pride.

"With a LOT of walking and running," Ollie added, laughing.

They told the others all about Leaf and Fang, about the rushing river and the baby mammoth, the cave lions, and the stampede.

"And look what Leaf gave us," said Tamiko, holding out the painted rock.

"That's a lovely piece of limestone," said Cheng approvingly.

"Not the rock," said Tamiko, laughing at the Geology Explorer. "The painting!"

"That's amazing," gasped Roshni.

"And already around eleven thousand years old," said Connor admiringly.

Tamiko carefully put the ancient painting inside one of the display cases, where everyone could see the details of Leaf's painting: her, and Ollie, and Leaf, and Fang, and the baby mammoth with his tiny raised trunk.

"Time to go home," said Ollie, yawning. "I am so tired!"

Tamiko realized that her own eyes were drooping, too. All around them, the walls of the Exploration Station lit up with glowing doors, ready to take the Explorers home.

"Bye, everyone!" the Explorers called, waving and each heading for a door. "See you next time!"

Tamiko felt the familiar whoosh of light and air as she stepped through her door. She blinked to clear the dazzle from her eyes. Yes! She was back where she had started, standing on the edge of the campsite in the mountains. She looked around for her mom, and realized she was still inside the tent.

Tamiko walked over to the cold campfire and studied it with a grin on her face. Moss, she thought. That's what we need. She found some scraps of dry moss and tucked them among the twigs at the bottom of the campfire, just the way Leaf had shown them. Then she picked up two hard-edged flints from the ground. She struck them against each other, holding them close to the moss. Yes! A spark leaped from the stones into the moss . . . and began to smolder.

She was blowing on the tiny flames when her mom emerged from the tent, holding the bag of marshmallows. Her eyes widened.

"Goodness!" she said. "How did you do that?"

Tamiko showed her mom the flints. "With a bit of Ice Age magic!" she said proudly.

MISSION NOTES

An Ice Age occurs when freezing temperatures cause ice to cover large parts of the world for a long period of time. Experts believe that the Earth has gone through five separate ice ages over its history.

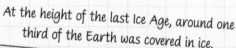

At the height of the last Ice Age, around one third of the Earth was covered in ice.

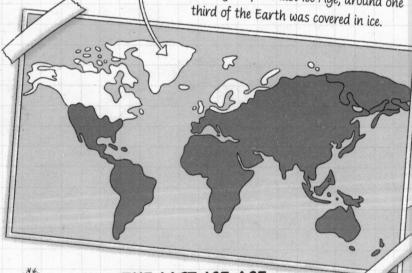

THE LAST ICE AGE

When people say "Ice Age" they usually mean the most recent one, which is also known as the "last Ice Age." It started about 100,000 years ago and ended around 11,700 years ago. It was during this Ice Age that mammoths walked the Earth.

LIFE IN THE ICE AGE

Like all living things, the humans that lived during the last Ice Age had to adapt to the cold. The people of the time were very dependent on hunting mammoths, deer, and other animals—not only for food, but also for clothing, tools, and shelter.

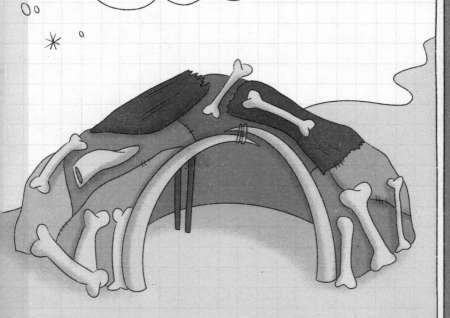

Humans on the mammoth steppe made structures from mammoth bones and covered them with animal skins to make huts to keep out the cold.

THE WOOLLY MAMMOTH

Woolly mammoths are the extinct relatives of modern elephants that lived during the last Ice Age.

Adapted for the cold

Unlike modern elephants, mammoths were well suited for cold environments. They had two layers of fur to insulate their bodies, cracks on the soles of their feet to grip the snow, and small ears to minimize heat loss.

Long, curved tusks

A mammoth's tusks could grow to about the length of a small car!

WHEN DID MAMMOTHS BECOME EXTINCT?

Most mammoths died off around 10,000 years ago, mainly due to being hunted by humans. However, a small number of them on a remote Arctic island survived until about 4,000 years ago—which means mammoths still existed when the ancient Egyptians built the pyramids!

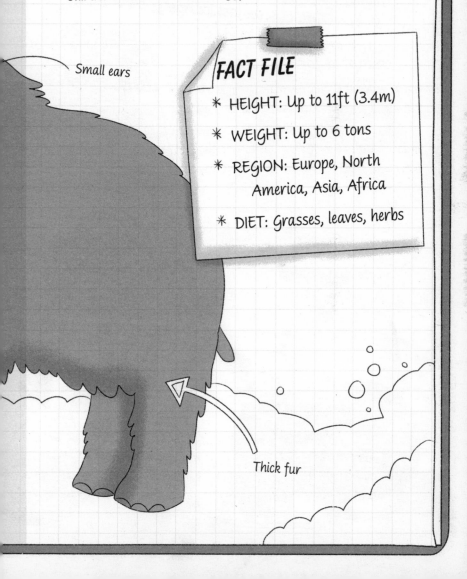

Small ears

FACT FILE

* HEIGHT: Up to 11ft (3.4m)

* WEIGHT: Up to 6 tons

* REGION: Europe, North America, Asia, Africa

* DIET: Grasses, leaves, herbs

Thick fur

MORE ICE AGE ANIMALS

Woolly mammoths weren't the only animals that roamed the mammoth steppe. It was also home to a wide variety of predators and prey—some of which are still around today.

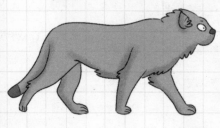

CAVE LION

Cave lions were the most fearsome predator of the time. Just like modern lions, cave lions lived in prides and hunted in groups.

STEPPE BISON

Steppe bison gathered together in huge herds to graze on the vast grasslands, much like the modern bison of North America.

MUSK OXEN

Musk oxen lived in quite small herds, and were often preyed on by wolves and other predators.

GOLDEN EAGLE

Just as they do today, golden eagles soared over the Ice Age plains searching for easy prey.

WOOLLY RHINOCEROS

Woolly rhinoceros were about the size of a modern white rhinoceros. They were covered in fur, and had a large hump filled with fat that helped them survive the cold.

SAIGA ANTELOPE

Saiga antelope were specially adapted to the cold. They still exist today.

QUIZ

1   What type of rock can be struck together to help start a fire?

2   True or false: The mammoth steppe was totally covered in ice.

3   What item do Tamiko and Ollie bring back to the Exploration Station?

4   True or false: Mammoths still exist today.

5   What group of animals does Tamiko scare off by luring them to fire?

6   True or false: The Ice Age came before the time of the dinosaurs.

7   Were mammoth tusks curved or straight?

Check your answers on page 127

GLOSSARY

ATV
An "all-terrain vehicle" that allows a rider to travel across various terrains. Also known as a quad bike

AUSTRALIAN OUTBACK
A huge, largely unpopulated area of Australia

BOTANY
The scientific study of plants

CAVE LION
An extinct type of lion that lived during the Last Ice Age

CONIFER
A cone-bearing tree with small needles

FLINT
A type of rock that can be used to make a spark. Flint was also commonly used in ancient times to make weapons and other tools

FURS
Clothes made from
the pelts of animals

HERD
A group of animals
that live and travel
together

ICE AGE
A period of time
when the world was
much colder, and
many parts were
covered in glaciers

MAMMOTH
An extinct relative
of the elephant that
had a shaggy coat
and curved tusks

MOSS
A type of small,
green, flowerless
plant

PREDATOR
An animal that
hunts and eats
other animals

SEDGE

A grasslike plant
that tends to grow
in cold locations

STAMPEDE

A group of
panicking
charging animals

STEPPE

The name given
to the vast, grassy
plains that stretch
from Eastern
Europe right across
central Asia

Quiz answers

1. Flint

2. False

3. A painted rock

4. False

5. Cave lions

6. False

7. Curved

For Zac and Oscar

Text for DK by Working Partners Ltd
9 Kingsway, London WC2B 6XF
With special thanks to Lucy Courtenay

Design by Collaborate Ltd
Illustrator Ellie O'Shea
Consultant Anita Ganeri

Acquisitions Editor James Mitchem
Designer Sonny Flynn
US Senior Editor Shannon Beatty
Publishing Coordinator Issy Walsh
Senior Production Editor Nikoleta Parasaki
Production Controller Leanne Burke
Publishing Director Sarah Larter

First American Edition, 2022
Published in the United States by DK Publishing
1450 Broadway, Suite 801, New York, New York 10018

DK, a Division of Penguin Random House LLC
22 23 24 25 26 27 10 9 8 7 6 5 4 3 2 1
001–327005–May/2022

A catalog record for this book is available from the
Library of Congress.

ISBN: 978-0-7440-5648-8 (paperback)
ISBN: 978-0-7440-5649-5 (hardcover)

Printed and bound in Great Britain by
Clays Ltd, Elcograf S.p.A.

For the curious
www.dk.com